SOME PERMANENT THINGS

JAMES MATTHEW WILSON

Wiseblood Books

Milwaukee, Wisconsin

Cover: Dominic Heisdorf

Printed in the United States of America
Set in Arabic Typesetting

Library of Congress Cataloging-in-Publication Data
Wilson, James Matthew, 1975-
Some Permanent Things/ James Matthew Wilson;
1. Wilson, James Matthew, 1975-
2. Poetry

ISBN-13: 978-0692258644
ISBN-10: 0692258647

To Livia Grace,

James Augustine,

and

Thomas Avery

New lives in this ancient and unsettled world

. . . too many among us are still looking at irrationality as the last bulwark of liberty.

—Etienne Gilson

TABLE OF CONTENTS

IV. TWO VERSE LETTERS

V. DISCIPLINE AND DESIRE

I

The Violent and the Fallen

The Mishawaka Cruisers

All wiry and cavern-chested, voices
Of rubber bands and spokes off bicycles,
The boys out late on West McKinley Ave.
Are waiting, talking, searching through the dark.

Their midnight-blue mesh jerseys are the fields
On which blank luminous 15s appear
In answer to the strokes of passing headlights.
A line of weekend cruisers, mufflers loose

And loud with bragging, makes its measured circuit
Along three blocks of neon fast-food chains,
The darkened panes of auto dealerships,
The Checks-Cashed, and the boarded Dollar Store.

A high-perched floodlight bathes in blinding milk
A fleet of new sedans and minivans
Beyond the cyclone fence. It's summer now
And light lives leaping in conic clouds of gnats.

Three boys follow my car as it gets trapped
Within the caravan, eyes settling for
My mute impatience in lieu of the hope
Of spying an unknown batch of girls with beer.

1

Their betters park mud-speckled muscle cars
And perch blunt, certain bodies on the hoods,
But these three wait with long legs, hairless, stretching,
Poked between high-tops and jean shorts. Above

Us, the sky opens into sweeping plains
That neither field nor parking lot, nor lights
Studded along the row of burning signs
Could penetrate or prettify. The sky

Is just an empty clearing for the heat,
And though these boys' hearts pound with want and weakness,
And though cars fill the street with chrome and order,
I catch the vacant boredom just beneath.

Just then, a gap forms as two girls hop out
From a green pickup's cab to join the crowd,
And I escape, turn right off the main drag.
Their eyes pursue my fenders, then turn back

In search of something worth the endless waiting.
I have a place to go, someone to meet,
But in their restless still-becoming rests
My own dread of the bare, the incomplete.

ALONE, FAR FROM *THE NEW YORKER*

A teenage boy, I'd flip its ad-hemmed pages,
    Its suave black columns, hoping there to learn
About the world of literary sages
    Who drank in wrinkled linen suits or turned

With cigarette to meet the camera's eye
    As if their lives consisted of genteel
Suffering in the heart's urbane mystery,
    Aborted love affairs, and drunken meals.

I memorized their names and read their books
    And tried to imitate the suited poses
That lent the writing life its charming look:
    A weary preference for Jameson over roses.

    I wrote stories; never heard, but listened for
    Cheever, Brennan or White's knock at my door.

BALLOON MAN

D'you know the sound balloon strings make when they been cut?
Tied to split knuckles, how they limply dangle there.
If Mac comes in and groans again and rubs his gut,
I'll say, "At least you got a job. The kids just stare

At me, and then up at the red, the rubbery green."
He knows the economics, so that's all I'll say:
Ten-thirty a.m. I give up and cut each string,
Then go to take a stool at Chuck's. If kids won't pay,

Then I don't gotta stand, a clown at the grocery
Until the sun has made my glasses steam and glare,
And I wish I could type or something. Who wants to be
A broken vendor day in, day out? Rotting there,

The stench of vulcan in your nose, the cheap twine cutting
Into your right hand's gritty reddening knuckles. The left
An only, last and loyal pal, its fingers clutching
The groaning flip-blade in its plastic-handled heft

To cut those unsold helium balls—the useless things.
  But Mac doesn't hardly sigh or swear at me no more,

4

Or ask, after I quit my work, if I will bring
A few bucks home from Chuck's. He knows that he has scored

Points on an old wound in the ribs that hurts like lime
Sizzling on my finger-cuts. I bow my head,
When he gets home from work, and wipe the tar and grime
That grocery parking lots have smeared on it. I'm dead,

Those little pimply brats say, when they come and gape
At me and the bright swelling sores of my balloons.
On a good day some brat with his allowance apes
Me, buys a green and blue, and I am flush by noon.

I don't care how they go, though it helps to sell, I guess.
    I'm neither lame nor small, I cannot sing a song,
But with a low and hungry swipe at her pink dress
My free left hand sends little Isabelle along,

Since she just like her mother talks too much. The rest
Stare from the corner of their eyes on the far curb.
Unless I start to scratch my sweating pits or chest,
Then they look wide and whisper something. I disturb

Grown women, but the brats come with their popsicles
As if I were a hobo clown fired from the circus,
To see if I'll bend down to take a few flung nickels.
Of course I will, the fricking kids. The things that hurt us

Most aren't the hard humiliations of a job,
Or knowing I'll never screw their ma's in their Festivas'
Back seat, but wondering if some other drooling slob
Has beat me to my stool and is shooting my tequilas.

    Mac knows that kind of man, though he will never be one.
He's got a girl, an Olds, in poker always *two*-pair,
While I take what I can, balloon man for this season,
Laughed at, but ready to bark, "Who *do* you think that *you* are?"

A View from the Studebaker Servants' Quarters

South Bend, Indiana

Between the house and yellowed, crumbling
Wall of the disused carriage house, a line
Of apple trees in blossom, grayed with rain,
Is "smoking" petals for the death of Spring.

Or *that's* the verb I found somewhere in Tennyson
To speak of a mediaeval April not
Unlike this one, with all the fertile rot
And antique bric-a-brac in the back garden.

The day is cold and a stone seraphim
Awaits with vine-wracked wings upon their flight,
Observing while he may the petals' white
Penumbra gathered in the grass's thin

Grip. There, it intersects with branches cast
Into a circular midday shadow: Volatile
Diagram sketched of silhouette and petals
Whose figure-eight weaves present, future, past,

In what has neither end nor origin.
I've milled about these trees for five months now,

While out to smoke a cigarette, and frowned
At wintering branches and the tasteless sin

Of wire fences, industrial concrete
Impinging on what otherwise might seem,
Not Eden, but some genteel type of dream.
Time has sullied taste till, save in discrete

Borders, most pastorals are just fantasy
These days. Nor can stone angels fill the role
Of resurrecting fearful miracles
From the tomb of three centuries' industry.

Between crass pessimism and my house,
The row of dwindling clouds of blossom stands.
Seventy years ago, there was a bland
Garden for servants here, and servants housed

In what are now my rooms. The novelty
Of English brick, kiln-baked tile, a view
Of that hunched mansion now called Tippecanoe,
Evoke this house's extinct pedigree.

With the decay of Studebaker and steel,
An age of maids and chauffeurs passed. South Bend
Became a town of decorous fortunes spent,
Where late-Victorian houses are "a steal."

So in this last fistful of years, new owners
Have tried with copied statues, period plants,
And trees that shed a vintage radiance,
To renovate this tomb to all that's former.

I've breathed its dust in, taken careful note
How plastic urns break in the snow; how I
Can merely mock at stone's sad history;
Pronounce its fate, perhaps, but just in quotes.

When sun is overhead and wind has blown,
A row of trees both green and bare with Spring
Will cast no shadow, and the petaled ring
Will have dispersed across the sinking ground.

LIVING TOGETHER

Where flecks of fabric tangle with your hairs,
Trimmed nails, the dry husks of dead beetles, bottle
Caps flipped into a corner off our beers,
There lies neglect and memory grown mottled

With light and wet air off the river; I,
Stretched out before the open window, watch
Its screen-diced luminescence occupy
The surfaces of mess. Though I can't touch

You now—you're out shelving books to pay the rent—,
The skein of dust before my level eye
Is your self with my own absently blent
In life's terse record: its sloughed but faithful sty.

Their Time Up at State College

It's hard to get your married brother drunk.
Now that you've reached the age he was once at
And he'll tell you for old time's sake how then,
After a night of shots and beer, he'd toppled
Down a hard flight of stairs. His future wife
Was there, she took him in her arms and slugged
Him off to bed, laughing at what he slurred,
Before; with combing fingers, held his head
Over the staircase rail. These two half-grown
Midwestern blond kids up at their state college.
She'd let him paint a flower on her cheek
That evening, right before she and the girls
Lit sweet cigars and found the room with booze.
After he'd let his stomach settle down,
They lay in the twin bed, his kelly jersey
With chipped-off number and once famous name
And her dry, painted cheek upon his chest.
They were young then and aren't so old just now,
And share this idly to identify
A bit with you, but don't begin to drink.
Your brother hasn't finished his first beer
And when you polish off your third, it seems
That you could never have a reckless time

A sugared time, as youthful time as they.
When they surrendered the age that you are now,
You lost it with them.

                    You have none at all:
No age, no wild youth to reflect on,
No half-remembered smiling anecdotes,
Nothing to joke about or to regret.
In present company, you are like them,
That is, you take their lives in listening.
To be as they once were, or as you are . . .

When somehow you, unlikable, shy you
Manage to find someone who can match drinks,
The mood turns maudlin and you let a sigh
Within the quiet bar you've ended at,
Looking across toward this anonymous
Partner, who can share nothing more than rounds,
You hesitate. Sip. And then begin
To tell those stories, near but not your own,
And far, quite far, from any time you know.

It's always fun to drink up at state college;
I've never been but so I've always heard.
My brother doesn't binge as he did then,
But she and him been married some years now.

They actually have a kid now. Want another.
Can you imagine that? And me an uncle.
It makes me shake to think about it, yeah,
So many people giving birth and so
Much wrong with this world. I can't understand
The war we're in. It's not my war. The war . . .

THE GYPSIES

On the margins of Tours

Comme je suis un étranger dans notre vie
        -Philippe Jaccottet

There is a fire beneath the trees, its smoke
   Threading through lumbering clouds and yellow-tipped leaves
In shades of settling night. My senses woke
   To madrigals tongued in the light of gypsies,

Their curious foreign sounds. At mid-June midnight,
   I see them sway before the fire, as if
A brood of curious drunks who've staggered in sight
   Of some town's decorous dances. Or, as if,

Desperate for company, they have grown cold
   And crouch about red coals of frantic talk,
To bear the winter freeze with stories told
   Largely by eyes and gestures. As I walk

   Back toward town, *my* words, *not* theirs, seem as those
   On whom all proper, shrugging doors have closed.

AT FATHER MAC'S WAKE

Saint Thomas Aquinas Church, 1987
Death found him upright in his chair, eyes shut.
He had retired a pair of years back, having
Forgotten at the altar to recite
The Creed—or skipped, again, some other part
That left us staring with mouths full of prayer
For which he'd left no room. The Church he built
In the brute modern style of a time
When everyone knew the face of Pius XII
And Paul VI was newly vilified,
Projected a wall of stained glass, with Christ,
Scientist, scholar, artist, engineer
Radiant in mosaic. The rising light
Would hit upon the cut shards, beaming inward
A sanctified view of American progress
Upon the sanctuary. All that went on
Without him; it wasn't necessity or failure
That weighed his death with sorrow, just the way
Those things more permanent than us retain
Meaning only in terms of what must pass,
And with the loss of memory even that passes.

Open Casket

I saw him sleep at the front of the church.
Had someone thought to smear a greasy thumb
Upon his forehead, say the prayer, and give
Him that last sacrament before his body
Calmed itself down to nothing? All the years
Of cold baptismal dunking, children crowding
Toward the confessional or to Communion,
The blaring organ and stone font's blunt head,
The dark three-chambered box with lights installed
Beneath his graven name, solemnities
Of wedding vows, new priests' first Masses after
Ordination—how many had he seen,
Before him from the altar, before him in
The pews? And now this one, who had seen all,
Seen through the darkness of the sacraments,
Was seen, and still, and silent in a box.

The Violence of Resurrection

I saw his folded hands upon the cross,
About the knuckles twined a rosary,
And Scottish plaid draped over the oak box
As if to cover his cold legs. But I
Was twelve, a little more, and had been led
To church that night and told to kneel, keep hushed,
When I could hardly bear to sit a minute

16

Without a sharp tug on my mother's skirt,
And asking, could we leave? My friends were out
Playing, and looked on absence as defection;
It was, in any case, not Sunday or
A holy day, but just another day.

Fr. Mac did not frighten me, but my
Father did and his look was all it took
To get my fingers knotted in reluctant
Prayer. So, I prayed to go outside, to shed
The clip-on tie, the navy slacks, the short sleeved
Dress shirt that was my uniform for school
And so were doubly inappropriate
In this, the freest of the summer months,
The longest days cut short by this long wake.

The casket lay a dozen feet before me.
I pressed my mouth against the humid lacquer
Thick on the pew, and with that stealing cowardice
Augustine tells us of, I drove my bike key
Into the wood as if to carve and scrape
Insignia of my envy and impatience,
My boredom, bitterness, and fresh despair.
And when my parents didn't rise, and when
Some young priest led us in a tedious hymn,
I prayed, "I don't believe in God; I don't

17

Believe in You," and waited for the chance
To file out into the yellow twilight
And never to come in that church again.
Now, in the foyer hangs a bronze relief
Of Fr. Mac above a cross of keys,
And those key-stabs I made may still be scarred
In the pew's aging wood, a seeming accident
That only I can read in memory:
Signs of a last attack before defeat.

The Vineyard Dinner: A Retrospect

She offered him the heart-meat of two doves,
The smoke and tartness of wine marinade.
It seemed he tasted her at one remove
And took with gratitude what she had made.

The smoke and tartness of wine marinade
Drifting across the vineyard, while they ate
And took with gratitude what she had made.
He set his fork and knife across the plate.

Drifting across the vineyard while they ate:
The bitter tannin rose from ripening grapes.
He set his fork and knife across the plate
And listened to the birdsongs sing of rape.

The bitter tannin rose from ripening grapes.
She offered him the heart-meat of two doves,
And listened to the birdsongs sing of rape.
It seemed he tasted her at one remove.

ET IN ARCADIA EGO

The evergreens haunt the vineyard's margin, encircling the bare
Truck-and-backhoe mangled hill from whose dry crest I stare

Across the lines of planted vines, in early spring; their dry
And lightening bark like chicken feet clutching at the sky.

The gravel spread about their husks reflects in crystaled gray
The inchoate heat the season brings educing each new spray;

And sour tar pearls dulled with dust bud on their fragile tendrils.
This is a time of promise and fear, an age that undoes men's wills,

And holds their eyes upon the living leaf, whose veined underside
Is death, and on these mildewed stakes, where fruit to rot is tied.

I too am here, it blurts in mud, it hums along the wires
Strung with notes of pinot noir, and gargles in the fire.

The cold wind cuts in from the lake. The season soon will turn
And, in its humid forgetfulness, prepare a darker turn.

ACEDIA

At the Civil War Memorial.
City Cemetery, South Bend, Indiana.

Some numinous thing I'd like to say, but guilt
    Before oracular high-flung sentiments
    Requires that what's been said is also meant,
And so my eyes cleave to the moldering silt.

Some miseries I'd like to offer witness,
    But that is not my blood-churned scalp, and not
    My shrapnel tiling the dust, and not
My father's gravestone unchiseled and unpolished.

The broken eaves of the green mansion bend
    Beneath the weight of snow and limbs, the crescent
    Of sky above its chimneys opalescent
With dry light, where all speech comes to an end.

  But who were these? These wraiths of singing bone
  Who knew Heaven's guilt and left me here alone?

Immigrant Serving Maid in Dublin

This morning in the tiled scullery,
    The sunk-eyed Romanian girl whose job it is
To serve the jetlagged tourists toast and tea,
    Stared out beyond the sugar cubes, cream tins,

And lumpy raisin scones, her arms set cross
    Her belly in an absent stewardship,
A chessboard apron falling at her waist,
    And no translatable word upon her lip.

Within her vagrant loneliness, the rushed
    Complaints at how the hotel breakfast tastes,
The momentary tourist's sneer, can't touch
    The boredom or the longing in her face;

    She's been borne here not on wings of desire
    But just to work and send home cash by wire.

FROM A BENCH IN ST. STEPHEN'S GREEN

I saw once a woman and a man
Turning their coffee mugs in hand
    Like two tense lovers pining;
Formica and the seated crowd
Smelling of hot beef, chattering loud
    Kept their arms from twining.

Their eyes were wrinkled, tired with age;
I'd not looked close enough to gage
    Their hard, serious murmur.
The woman wore a pendant heart;
The man showed her accounts and charts,
    As fits an estate lawyer.

Hence this girl on a bench with me
Would seem my bodied intimacy
    To one on a walk passing.
And by my smile at her words
He'd think what I'd desired heard
    Like the sounds of undressing.

Perhaps the lawyers called to bar,
The strollers strolling in the park
    Are equal to their seeming.

But in my frustrate polite blush
Lingers no knowledge of her touch
    Or satisfactory meaning.

II

VERSE LETTER TO MY FATHER

The artisan, in the normal type of human development and of truly human civilizations, represents the general run of men. If Christ willed to be an artisan in a little village, it is because He wanted to assume the common condition of humanity.

—Jacques Maritain

Their God is their stomach; their glory is in their "shame" . . . He will change our lowly body to conform with his glorified body . . .

—Philippians 3:19, 21

You will remember better than I can
The mealy smells of woodchips, earth-chilled concrete,
And laundry from the other room, which crept
Into your basement workshop; and the long, neat
Pile of timber laid out for my desk.
Over the course of my sixth year, you built
It, towering, wide with bookshelf, drawers and cabinets;
And carved the front with gratuitous leafy frills,
As any old woodworker would have done,
As if the dead planks from an unknown tree
Should own as artificial scars the forms
They would in nature bear but never be.
Our house was filled with pottery and glasses,
The other desks and chairs and tables you'd
Crafted for other sons at other times.
But this one stood in ornate solitude
Behind the furnace, waiting for your brush
To darken the blond grain an oaken brown,
To sand its splintered crest and joiners smooth.

You left the radio on when not around—
At work perhaps, or mowing the lawn outside.

And I would look up at its half-hewn form,
Hear the roar as the mower reversed outside,
And sense, from damp and sawdust, something born.

It was too big, of course, not for me then,
But for the house. You scraped the walls and marred
The fresh-stained surface trying to get it
Upstairs and into place with my toy cars,
My Star Wars people, bed and crucifix,
All the accouterments of childhood.

Though everyone said it was beautiful,
Though you rubbed soap along the drawers, I could
Never get them open with any ease,
Nor did I, as the years passed, start to write
My homework there. It turned into a crypt
Of sorts, for rock and coin collections, kites
And comic books, the model tanks you built
Because I'd neither patience nor the will
To glue such minute replicas together.
Nonetheless, when guests turned up, I was thrilled
To show this master trophy of your mastery
And stare on it myself in admiration.

Though it was sold three years ago, I see
It as a great gift, symbol and occasion.
For where it stood, and stands now still in memory,

It staked a claim as faulted monument
A biochemist in his off-hours made
Sure of intention if not measurements.

　　You are the person who has taught me most
Of various kinds of doing and of making.
And when you left your workshop idle, you
Furnished as well a symbol of unmaking.
Pardon me, Father, if it's you I choose
As guide, as I ask our world's curious features,
What is a well-made thing, and how to make
An artifice out of the things of nature.

II

　　Not given to the free flights of ideas
Or words, (I almost hear) you brush aside
The arguments on every current cause—
Abortion or assisted suicide,
Or those more recent, more minute affairs
The harvesting of cells from embryos—
Impatiently, the scientific terms
Whip-stitched together in a bland picot
Intimidating as ornate. You knew
The lawful nature of the physical,
And so interrogated what we'd do

29

With a criterion both strict and clinical.

 Outside the trained world of the scientist,
Agreement on what nature is seems less
Settled; perhaps because it's not the circle
In which thought spars, the unsaid terminus
That you, in white coat, staring down through glass,
Would seem not to arrive at, but begin
With—with the almost shrugging modesty
Of one to whom this much, no more, is given.

 I think of Rousseau, who thought nature was
All that was wild, uncultivated, raw.
What man had made, nature was not. A horror
Rattled through him at every chain he saw.

 To this, de Maistre replied with purging fire.
That which exists, if not divine, is caught
Within the ceaseless nature of becoming:
All that is tells us nothing of what *ought*
To be. He dreaded barbarous man would dare
Think his confounding of the True and sense,
The aching stomach and the smoking meat,
For every judgment sufficient evidence.

 A boy, he wrote, will hold within his palm
A new-hatched sparrow; he'll touch the down and beak
And clutch it closer in a cage of fingers,

Until he feels the flutter of bones break.
If nature was an all encompassing brute
Crushing in power and mortality,
Then goodness lay in the unnatural act
Of slavish turning to authority.

   To these Gauls, let me add an Englishman,
The prototypical conservative
Who saw in raised chivalric sabers, alpine
Peaks an ethical imperative.
Burke said that nature *of itself* was cruel,
But deep in root, in sap, in spreading leaf
A tender hope refined itself and grew
With absentminded slowness. In his brief,
The counter-entropy of custom and
Tradition played their juvenating part.
Cultures and governments must grow as trees;
No contradiction there: man's nature is art.

III

   I know if you were here right now, you'd grimace
At all this academic embarrassment
Of talk. But since you're my only reader, please,
Let your insouciant son follow his bent.
   Excurses such as Burke's are predicated

On nature as a kind of constancy.
But it, by definition, changes always;
The lapping waves throw up their potency
On actual sands. That endless mortal throb
Of dark descending where land slips to sea.
We've lived so long in earshot of the protest
Against such fate, our oldest poetry,
That verse seems a dead letter written to
The dead. But I write now to ask a lingering
Question of you.

            Do you remember when,
Some news show on some humid summer evening,
When twilight lingered hours at the screen
Door; and some late-returning neighbor mows
His grass, its heavy smell, drifting inside
Along with the more faint mosquito drones?
You sat in your chair, I sprawled on the floor,
A plastic soldier fighting in my hands,
And all our light came from a slipping sun,
Or in the television's blue-fingered bands.
On screen, with masked voice and a shadowed face,
Some creature told of how a surgeon's hand—
With scalpel, thread, the unimaginable—
Made look a woman what had been a man.

The shy shame of the unknown face collided
With an electric voice speaking a need,
Not just to have done what was done, but tell
Of metamorphosis with such a greed
For details I could grasp but not comprehend.

    Later, I wanted to ask what it meant.
But curiosity fell off in shame,
And that became just another incident
To rhyme with others later, so that sound
Seemed to mean more darkly without discernment.
Years have passed. We have superannuated
Shame with tabloid pages, our natural ferment
Has melted, not eschatologically,
But rather in consumer honeyed hives,
Where nature now is subject to revision.
T.V. shows men who've become wives of wives,
Their broad unsuited faces in ill-fitting
Clothes. Conscientious objectors in a war
Tiresius tried to table in his myth,
No god could force them to stay what they are.
The screen's profuse with other shows, where girls—
Less monstrous, far more trivial—resign
Their modest forms, thinking fairytales
Come true through plastic surgeons' slick designs.

Doubtless, the shill's embrace of television
And medical technique has much to do
With how frequent these transformations are.
But not all take place in the light of noon,
Where stage lights and a viewing audience seem
To give with their attention their approval;
The vain unconfident seek tummy tucks,
Nose jobs, and any kind of hair removal.

Father, this world that you can understand
By Chemistry, yet, as one more private being
Unsure what right or leash a public power
Could wield to cleave the flesh from market scene;
Tell me, have we become more deformed monsters
By Shelleyean ambitions or by vice?
Are grafts and pelvic scars the only fruit
Of natural science grown to artifice?

IV

Those rare nights, Father, when we sit across
The table from each other eating our
Suburban dinners in a house of beige,
Within that quiet privacy of hours
We hear, like tumblers slipping in the locked
Back door, a TV drama's children of

Divorce, their pierced and tattooed proclamations
They recognize no outside or above.
They've claimed their bodies as the cowboys claimed
The West: with clumsy rhetoric, barbed wire.
You stare down at your plate, without reply,
Biding the hours till you can retire.

   I would be silent too. The ownership
Of houses, all that talk of men and castles,
Long ago slipped into the market place,
Decreed that brains and bowels were but vassals,
The merchandise of our unruly wills.
Your body's *yours*, just as this poem is mine:
To make, destroy—a tenancy of will,
For every citizen and concubine.

   Creations of a world we helped to make;
That stripped chicken bone on the gravied plate
Betrays us as the beneficiaries
Of terms that, without Terminus, now grate.
So this embarrassed quiet and the question:
Can we untangle chtonic wants and bodies
From the stretched net of private property?
Or has the gleam of television, shoddy
And obvious as it sometimes seems, made all
Things, real and false, true or imagined, turn

Monochrome, till appearances are all,
And all things can be ours, if we just learn
The necessary digital techniques?

   With Wellesian aplomb, our journalists ask
If fiction can be passed off as pert fact.
But surgeons, salesmen have taken up the task,
Just like a mirror, of making fantasies
As actual as your own actual skin.
Which must be why some artists throw their shit
Or sperm upon a canvas; however thin
The charge, they want us—we who dine—to feel
The shock of the real. Such crude artifice
I've tried to stay from sundering this poem,
To offer sense, rather than ugliness.
But following Horace, I have had to note
Neatly the very monsters that I fear.
If they embarrass both of us, at least
They're only words, not spectacles in clear
And gaudy color, road signs on a path
Of nature, warning of inglorious ends.

   And that, in truth, is what our nature is:
The course from birth to death that we must wend
To be mere human beings; no set of laws
Gleaned watching wild dogs rutting in a wood,

But what we learn from living through our doing
In exodus from goods to final good.
Burke almost had it right. Just as this meter
Grew gradually out of native English stress;
Just as the cut of fabric and the stitch
Must match the body's contours if a dress
Of worm-spun silk or suit of gabardine
Are to be worn with any elegance;
Hence to the rhythm of our lives we learn
The steps and missteps that become its dance.

 Now, Father, at the sight of ownership,
Don't wither in the silence shame induces.
Our oldest concepts have their applications
As well as modern and antique abuses.
I, like de Maistre's boy, have grown up, discerned
Authority of a supernatural
Order shows much—but only to complete
The proper order in the human halls
We each pace leaving echoes in our wake.
And so we find that the grip of our pleasure
Need not choke everything it can, but may loose
The fist of art to fit the palm of nature.

—2001

III

LA ROCHEFOUCAULD'S GHOST

To The Reader

Others taunt me with fleeing reality;
I find in wells, most often, something more
Than white dumb stones numbed to eternity.

When I write verse on the heart's or mind's core,
I take it that there's something there to find
Beyond the pulp on the material floor,

Though to speak of it seem sunlight to the blind.
Is Order just to caulk wood boats with pitch,
As if a sea-fit craft were false design?

To gloat in chaos, spite the native itch
To cut through mobbed obscurity and grasp
The rational sense waiting within; to stitch

An ugly patch-work shawl with broken clasps
Instead of learning skilled embroidery
That makes a fine and useful coat to last

Beyond the hour: such cynical strategies
Seem opium for anxious but weak minds.

Baudelaire writes that Nature's company

Has commerce with the intellect, which winds
Through that *expansion des choses infinies.*
For him, the senses were a means to find

Where things and their ideas meet ethically.
But to detail the truth in decadence
Is not the only task—or shouldn't be.

He swooned in details, and died in consequence,
Unwilling to hear the lesson in his words.
One ought to note and weigh the relevance

Of those undying shades signaled in words,
Taking them both as beauties and as guides,
Rowing the ship of heart and mind with words.

Good fortune has not blown me to collide
With the toothed rocks of which some poets sing.
And though it costs, I refuse to elide

A reasonable world, whole and discrete,
Or let the only language I compose
Mumble the bitch that "things aren't always neat."

With humble hand, I've set here words in rows,
Printed such lines in the effort to entice
The reader see the world an ordered rose.

If this gets called in turn "genteel" or "nice,"
"It lacks the flavor of burnt toast and shoestrings,"
Know all I'd meant to do was be precise.

We cannot learn from drugged hues, violent spewings;
Or wrestle truth ensnared in proud confusion,
Where doggerels arrogant and obese go strewing

The talkative forest limbs in hysteric ruin.
I've said this world makes perfect sense to me.
And if my ghostly ancestors-in-allusion

May show their numbered knowledge, then we'll see
If, having learned their pattern, you don't agree.

DRINK, DRINK

After Baudelaire

One must get drunk. One must *always* be drunk,
For in its haze hides every longed-for thing.
To numb yourself to leaden time which breaks
Its weight upon the back, and slowly brings
Your corpse to crawl, mired in the dirt, you must
Come drink without repose. But drink of what?

Of wine, or poetry, or virtue—such
As you prefer, so long as you drink enough.

And if sometime on the steps of Versailles;
Or lounging near some flowered ditch; or closed
In your room's torpid shade, you suddenly
Awake, your mind half-cleared and turned morose,
A furious joy now vanished. Ask the wind,
The stars, the waves, the birds, the clock, and all
That wanders, sings, creates, or speaks or shines.
Ask these what time it is and they will all
Reply. The stars, the wind, the waves, the dark birds,
The clock's pinned, grinding hands will answer you:

"It's time to drink if you would not be martyred
In Time's dull coliseum. But quickly choose

Your wine, or poetry, or virtue—such
As you prefer, so long as you drink enough."

London, 1841
The loudening clop of hoof on stone
Echoes beyond the boneyard gates.
He ignores this, dug three feet down,
Wool trousers dank with sod; too late

For caution at the tired cabman's
Squint eyes. His own eyes strain, back bent
Into steel wedging dirt. Then chapped hands
Grub for wood without a lamp's glint.

San Francisco, 1998
A fortyish bearded man with eyes
Glaucous from finding that *The Globe*
Panned his memoir: "A tale of wives
Divorced and bees in confessional mode.

It seems not life, but prolix lines
Of scrawled notes from an afternoon
Spent reading Darwin." His shirt lies
Stretched on his futon's back. The room's

Air, bone-dry, nips the stain where he
Rubbed soap and water: lost in dreams
Of dying bees, he'd spilled his tea,
For which that press made curdled cream.

London

It serves a use to disentomb
What hasn't any soul left. Hair,
Like silver thread fallen from a loom;
Bone; pile of nails. Dust spumes like a pair

Of black wings on a crushed moth, when his
Shovel stabs through the rotted wood
Of a coffin lid. He stoops and wrenches
The upper door wide, its fresh-bored

Hole seems a window meant to serve
The sockets of this smiling cracked skull—
As if it lost with flesh, its nerve.
He stoops to scavenge up his bag-full.

San Francisco

After her marriage, Mother haunted
Funerals incessantly.
He'd written back to her: he wanted
Imagination's faculty

To proximate her deceased mind,
Explaining why she'd dragged him there.
Strachey and Frazer helped him find,
In ritual, necrotic fear.

He dissects all. His memoirs are
A history of bland neuroses
Who think they're dust in underwear.
He writes, *she saw in graves, sweet roses.*

London

"I've done no wrong. It's just my business,"
He calls toward the caretaker's fan
Of dangling light. From this armed witness,
He shades his face with soiled hands.

What noble, fine excuses he'd
Absorbed, listening to the edicts
Of his employer, now recede
From mind: those long, confusing secrets

He scarcely comprehends, *to advance*
Science; knowledge's skeleton
Is not abstract, but in these time-blanched
Bones . . . In his fear, he's dropped his puns.

They crumble, as the coffin lid
Dissolves beneath this crime's arrest.
The light and thief sprawl on a quid
Of collarbone in a rotted vest.

NEVERMORE

After Paul Verlaine

Old dreams, old images, what do you want with me?
In Autumn, when the thrush falls in the vacant air,
And the sun slaps her rays down—a dull monocular
Vision of yellowing wood kissed farewell by the breeze—

We walked, in solitude with one another, dreaming,
She and I. Our thoughts, like her hair, blew in the wind.
Just then, she turned her trembling eyes on me and in
A voice of vibrant gold asked, "What gives this life meaning?"

So broken and deep-ringing, that angelic tone!
A weak smile was all I could give—and that alone,
Before I kissed her whitened hand in dedication.

The first flowers with such levity give up their scent;
And so it seemed, with its enchanting susurration,
The evanescent *yes* she never said but meant.

NOT YET, NOT YET

My Father, you know all I've done before
My conscience drinks to sleep or can restore
Its equipoise with quick forgetfulness.
You felt my drunk hand pulling off her dress,
Her warm breasts rising in the bedroom light,
And watched her give herself up to my sight.

My mouth wakes stale and dry. A wine glass turned
Upon its side has stained the rug. I turn,
Discovering her, who's fallen in my bed
And slept beyond my waking. What had I said
To get her here? And was she, last night, *was* she
More beautiful, her sleep-lined face more lovely?
Did that thick red-brown hair done up in pins
Seem worth the slop of sheets we've ended in?

Yes, Father, you know how I'll try excuse
Those naked hours: how talk and bourbon loose
Another self in me and girls like this
With beings as brief and piercing as a kiss;
How I'll recall the white spread of her thighs

As I overshadowed them, and with a cry
Of formulaic and familiar prayer
Will try to clothe their motions from your stare.
But as I see her out, unnamed and lonely,
Her smoked throat hoarse, the daylight thick with honey,
Of last night's furtive touch could you remind me?

BUNCHES OF BLACKBERRIES

After Francis Ponge

The poem constitutes a typographic
Thicket along a road that neither leads
Outside of things nor stretches to the spirit.
On certain sorts of winding vines there breeds

A congeries of spheres that take their tint
From a minute yet heavy drop of ink.

Black, rose, and beige, clustered in bunches, they
Sooner suggest a spectacle like some
Red clan of sundry freaks than some sweet free
Temptation waiting to be picked. Now come

To see the disproportion of seed to pulp,
Most birds but ill-appreciate the taste just
Because so little meat remains once gulped
And passed at arduous length from beak to anus.

The poet out on his professional walk
Finds food in them for contemplation, though.
"It is," he speculates in private talk,
"Successful in a set of carefully sowed

Labors unusual for a fragile flower."
Although one pass through grim entanglement
With threatening thorns to pluck their modest power,
Wild blackberries reach a patient denouement

Of perfect ripeness in the very same way
This poem, or any poem, must be made.

LYRIC

A light began to tremble on the horizon of his mind. He was not so old—thirty-two. His temperament might be said to be just at the point of maturity. There were so many different moods and impressions that he wished to express in verse.

No different than a little cloud
All puffed with sun-delighting corners,
Molting face and limb and shroud
Down an aisle of sky—new-born, or

Newly dead, minute by minute—
The clutching hand carves characters,
Then stanzas, though there's nothing in it
Save for the gazer with his sure

Seat in the solitary field
That tremors, trembles, registers
The unheard mines and guns, but yields
Them no quarter, mourns but will not stir.

No different than the craft of kettles,
The scalded metal speaking heat,
Or of extracting slivers and nettles
As one pitch cry admits defeat;

Than steady hands that knot the black tie
And button the black suit when bidden
To come and kneel before the cracked high
Altar where coffined hopes are hidden.

LIONEL JOHNSON

The other day, my hunger for and trust in
Authority led me to read Augustine.

Meaning, he writes, is time's intensity:
The fragile point (where thought and act coincide,
No longer passing moments separately
Allotted) rests beyond time's tick and guides
It. For a moment, I felt, not its pulse,
But, an immobile stasis held my heart.
While sin and snow and ocean waves convulsed
I saw it whole—time and space without parts—
That is the end of every thought.

ERNEST DOWSON

                                        Not so.

Glass voices clank and shatter in a darkness—
Or dark it's called because they claim to know
Only what's present—edifying light
Must come from elsewhere, if at all. The wood
Is shadowed only when a match ignites

A cigarette like a dying star. "Why would,"
They ask, "a sane man suffer your hard way?
We pass our vigil like a round of drinks,
And keep our pleasure in our stomachs. What day
Have you enjoyed so much as we? Endowed
With polished moments like a tide-washed shell,
We drink and eat and pay the rising rent,
Keep hunger down until our cash is spent."

So come with me into a dimming room
Which doesn't "mean," but like a match consumes.

LIONEL JOHNSON

Leave, rather. Feel your hunger's deeper thrust,
Subject it to the reason that you trust,
And thus be sane. You know that both were sent
For ends beyond this finite feast. These, bent
On certain pleasures that would give the flesh
A nervous liveliness but mock the rest
Given in the true bread and the red wine
On which the saints once and forever dine.

Find your way out before the rattling door
Slams shut against the wind and creaks no more.

W.B. YEATS

I couldn't agree more, Lionel, one must flee
This stifling darkness into one more deep,
Where flesh finds the source of its mystery.
I've sometimes thought, perhaps, such wisdom creeps
Among those ghosts who lie entombed at New Grange.
Come with me, both of you. Let's go and hear
What truths the dry bones chant beyond the mute range
Of reason till our bodies disappear.

I have a long life yet to live and fear
That once we've heard, I'll have to leave you there.

Beyond Gibraltar

So many years ago it hardly bears
   Remembering, the Babbitts and the Wilsons
Of slight yet dignified New England swore
   That pedantry, by half, was the worst treason.

Oh, pack one's sentences with portmanteaux
   One may, or muse on botany by lamplight.
But don't fling wide the case of what one knows.
   It would give any sensible girl a fright

To see one smiling in the dark upon
   The walls cocooned with butterflies in glass.
But one dull girl I know protests each turn
   Of phrase, all dancing wit. She would've harassed

   The Tuscan: "C'mon, Alighieri, don't you know?
   It's *Odysseus*! And the facts say he went home."

Yeats in London

Here he sits, scribbling of black pigs and fate,
Of time and Twilight tales, that bare broomstick
Blavatsky called stout Protestants come late
To bite and tear away the briars thick

With Catholic degeneration: notebooks filled
By thoughts transformed to symbols. Through the glass
All London roils in thickening fog whose still
Obscurity seems like a gnostic masque

Where all he won't believe may still be seen:
A vision's second-hand remembering
    That shames the cold room's bare walls.

His Da, stirred

In anger from his studio, where each brush
Stroke re-inscribes the real, sighs now, "You're just
    A poet, Willie, no philosopher."

SOME MAXIMS FOR SAMUEL SEWALL

With lines from La Rochefoucauld

I

Hypocrisy's the homage vice pays virtue,
The politician says in public penury.
  But fools desire wisdom in solitude,

And so he airs his shame while making way through
The crowd of newsmen with their cameras whirring.
Hypocrisy's the homage vice pays virtue.

  They'd thought to catch his blush for the late news,
To scapegoat him before a hungry jury.
  A fool desires wisdom in solitude,

But never taller seemed the fallen Gertrude
When she confessed the fault that she had married.
Hypocrisy's the homage vice pays virtue.

  Unburdened of his shame, at last, he views
Them as a murder of crows who stab at bird seed.
  A fool desires wisdom in solitude,

But those of neither sin nor merit brood
On others', wish they'd fare to board the ferry.
Hypocrisy's the homage vice pays virtue.
    A fool desires wisdom in solitude.

                    II
The balance of the wise is merely art
Such as that violinists work on strings.
To shut off agitation in the heart

Is much neglected now; we'd rather start
Confessing to see what reward it brings.
The balance of the wise is merely art,

So adolescents choose their wounds *à la carte*;
Far better to be "natural" than serene.
To shut off agitation in the heart

Will hardly do. The corpses in the yard
Must crawl again, and patched pipes new leaks spring.
The balance of the wise is merely "art,"

As in repression, fraudulence—a part
For posing stoics in a play who mean
To shut off agitation in the heart.

An age given over to therapeutic farts
Looks on the decorous or brave and "zings,"
The balance of the wise is merely the art
To shut off agitation in the heart.

III/ Envoy
My eyes have fallen from eternity
To idle on that wit civility
Can teach a man to know with other men:
The light tread of the pithy through the den.

Since Sewall, from his pulpit, confessed his wrong
In riling Salem's blistering, zealous throng
To violence, one's dismayed—put off, at best—
By gnostic nostrums from a haughty chest.

So, let us savor common sense's cream
And leave dense curds for cloistered monks to dream.
It was such dreaming, after all, they say,
That got the witches burned, the heretics flayed.

Although we once asked much of reason's prodigies,
We're better off with smartly worded modesties.
If they seem trifling, they are human themes,
At least, so take them thus, these terse *Maximes*.

ESSAY ON EDUCATION
W.E.B. Dubois Library

In the reading room, I stoop before
A battered *Essais* by Montaigne,
And hear a man's hoarse voice complain.
His hushed, agreeing friend sits there,

Imbibing an impolitic plea:
He hates all law and government.
No one ever asked his consent.
He wants his freedom instantly.

I think of all the shelves in chambers
Packed dense with books; and how they got
Written, published, preserved not
By chance, but through labyrinthine labors.

The book before me is in French.
I struggle reading, but remember
How long it was, and how much harder
To learn my native tongue—and once

That starts, you're never really done.
How strange a place to plot anarchy:
Where a strict wisdom seems to be
Both freedom's guide and what it's won.

Though languages and libraries
Are not themselves an education,
They have for it often been mistaken.
I too dislike complacencies,

And were material monuments
Its essence rather than its measure,
Perhaps I would indulge his pleasure
In ultramontane violence.

To N.H.

The world's more difficult than any text.
   I see the working people in their scrubs
Or coveralls, smoking near some multiplex
   For cat-scans, dental crowns, and rehab. rubs—

For every service that can't be delivered
   Into a cellular suburb's house of glass.
Some months ago, a woman whom I'd never
   Give half my heart, set my arm in a cast.

If all such functionaries can perform
   Set tasks with mute and measured competency,
Why should the writer of a dozen poems
   Mimic their minds' surplus simplicity

   Instead of specializing every bit,
   Like them, in one skill: cold, allusive wit?

OF CORRESPONDENCES

After Baudelaire

The living columns girding Nature's halls
    Whisper, descant, or flash dense knotted words;
Man walks amid these runic forested walls,
    Finds welcome in their intelligible accord,

Their myriad echoes bounding till suffused
    Into a deep and verdant unity.
All tones and voices twine in air that moves
    With the perfumes of night, the stench of day:

Unfaded scent from off an infant's skin,
An oboe's music soft, a lush field's green—
The stuff of riches, rot, glory and sin,
Expands and binds all things, seen and unseen,

    Till amber, musk, invisible incense,
    Anoint the embrace of intellect and sense.

THE BOOK OF NATURE I

I'll tell you, it's a lovely spring:
My windows papered in the mauve
    Of blistering clustered buds;
The air, ripe with cut earth, slow-moves
    Noiseless against the glass,
    And the sky hasn't found its bright sting.

I'll tell you, it's a shrouded spring,
Where rain has scuffed the darkness up
    And petaled the raw mud.
Thunder startles the teacups
    And floods them in the grass
    All sharp with shadow shards and lightning.

I come to tell you everything:
Articulate the season's print,
    Storm's moralizing thud.
I spell out light and dark, each hint,
    In hope that mind might pass
    From florid things to fruitful meaning.

When *New York Times* and English Queens
Blow down the dust-blind blanching road,
    Where *is* can't reach to *should*,
And faces gawk like empty nodes,
    I join the blossomy Mass,
    In which day answers our deep pleading.

BARNUM

That is of course the Catholic tradition—saturnalia
that can end in a moment, like the crack of a whip.
                              —Ford Maddox Ford

After the clowns and seals, and the trapeze
Had swung its sequined fare into the dark,
Out came on one ornate tiered pedestal
The living statues. Their skin painted gold

To the edge of each lapid eyelid's line,
Rendering mortared metal, human flesh
One substance, their mundane distinction rubbed out
As some cosmetic blemish lost in gold.

They had crossed into terra incognita,
To some small workshop where Pygmalion
Could chisel them just one stroke beyond life
Upon a raised and lighted plinth of gold.

The statues ground their gears or slow joints
From poses where their tendons strained for stillness,
To long deliberate movements, more concrete
In beauty than a banker at his gold,

As if, in his dimmed world of greed alone
The heart's debased by metal's pressing weight.
Silence replaced wild whistles in the crowd
As a thin molded dryad with her gold

Back arching stretched away from the circled earth;
The central man, her Atlas, lifted her
Into an airy orbit far from ores
Of hate and hunger in the daily sweat for gold.

Another man rose on his broadening back,
On one of pure strength, two formed wings in risen
Immobile flight, till three were one again:
A single, hammered trinity of gold.

That spectacle of union in the comic
Ring did away with mocks or tragedy,
Dispensed with all our sloppy narratives,
Forgot our fall and raised men into gold.

THE BOOK OF NATURE II

The caterpillar grass
   Bleaches into its withered winter stasis;
The shadows of the fall's last spiders pass
   Into still, secret places.

Gravity has woven
   An umber bed of needles off the pines
That ring this acre, dried in a drought's oven,
   Which intimates some divine

Refusal to send rain.
   The needles pile like finger nails of those
Left, by authoritarian neglect, their pain,
   Their sweating woolen clothes,

To scratch at walls for seasons
   In the unworlded silence of a cell.
That is, the exercise of prowling reason
   Draws from this scene the hell

Of other days, discovers
    In the ashen curlicues of dormant vines
The nervous script of executed brothers
    Left dead along the lines.

This landscape is a poem,
    Forced back, retreated from the universe
To a depleted page's acreage, blown
    Into a hairline verse.

All that was once discerned
    In the created text of the plowed earth,
The rough-etched fractures of the sea, the turned-
    Out, sweetened afterbirth

Of isles of ripening fruit
    Has been exiled. Appetite paves it over,
Erects a store for armaments or men's suits,
    Or den for casual lovers.

Having such command,
    At last, imposing as he wills and does,
He makes a silent courtesan of the land
    To free her of other cause.

Despite him, reason seals
   This vision of a pine-ringed field within
The world as its indelible and real
   Mute book of blood and skin.

Dark Places

You stare into the azure distances
    That eyes cannot exceed.
    A serious voice bleeds
Through the wall, but you don't hear what it says.

At night, you fold the paper in your lap
    To solve the crossword; as
    Descending letters pass
Onto the page, you sense a code, perhaps

A whole vocabulary, meant for you
    That you may never speak.
    The bedroom windows creak
As if your mother, three years dead, brings news.

The real repels our words or swallows them.
    All we can do is point
    In agony, anoint
In ecstasy our stuttering intent:

The sky's bright emptiness reduced to phrases
  Imploding definition;
  Beyond concise confessions,
The coins, carved bones, and blood brought from dark places.

DE PROFUNDIS

After Raïssa Maritain

God, oh, My God, the space between us I cannot endure.
Reveal to me that pilgrimage both absolute and pure,
That pathway without wreckage, of my soul into Your heart,
Unlike those men chart on the earth in measurable parts.
My soul is plucked and poor, and feels the wound of everything
In its unspeakable slap, and with its all too human ring.

Pain ravished me of my first years.
And now, I'm just a ghost that goes out moaning for its marrow
Along roads hard and narrow
That hope has forced on it with tears.
In justice, my eyes rise toward You, beneath a loneliness
Whose shadows—dark as headstones, bloodied altars—
          weigh and press.

How can I come to you beyond the obscurity of signs,
To meet in flesh the light of Your Word without going blind?
All that is said of You is sacrilege—and what You say
Yourself in our tongue hides in mottled deeps of mystery.
For, while You shroud Yourself in speaking darkness or withdraw,
The world You fashioned coruscates with stars that overawe,
And the abyss in which You set them terrifies my soul.
From those abyssal depths, I cry to You, My God, my goal.

OLD MAN IN A CAFE

Imagine, like a student who has come
Across a still-life of a pair of boots
In the back gallery of a museum,
That this man, sitting here before you, has
A fold of bills tucked in one of his shoes,
Between the argyle sock and leather upper,
The rubber soles worn crooked, the left one cracked
And smelling of the pavement's wormy damp.

Because there are no places fit to shield him,
Where the wide streets and awnings blanch with sun,
The park rain-washed, and slick grass hissing on
The heels of children uniformed, fatherless,
Four o'clock darkness hides him and his papers
Spread out to show the trading numbers, there,
Ill-suited to the buzz of frothing milk.

For you who think he meditates on fact,
The memory of finance, the largess
Hidden behind what greasy wool he wears;
For you who see his lips are brown with coffee
And think him but a pensioner whose fall
Though hardly interesting was at least sad;

Like all the indigent and muttering,
Let him be counted no such easy figure.

    But say instead, if he has lost all grace,
He had his share. If he no longer speaks,
His language, like as not, was eloquent
Once. Give him at the least these fumbling words,
And count him not as typical of an age,
Of one particular time, but as the late
Twilight which any suited breast must find,
Fallen quiet with the lapse of history.

    And then consign, along with caricature,
This imagistic obverse charity
To the blank coffee darkness of unknowing,
Those places where what's there cannot be said.

"And Beat Upon This High Cloud of Unknowing"

After a hard trek up loose rocks, I found
    Myself not far below the peak, chest gasping
And staggering on my legs. The fog had swallowed
The path behind; my memory was hollow
    Where your and others' names belonged, where last spring's
Acanthus blooms perdured. I fell to the ground.

I may have slept an hour, I don't know.
    But when my eyes turned upward, they felt pressed
By the weight of a cloud that blotted all,
Enshrouded all in that strange dark. I called
    Into the raveling air. My sight grew less
The more I strained for light, while I struck blow

On blow against the black, whose insubstantial
    Vault resonated like a drum of steel.
You'd not have recognized my voice. It cried,
"Just let me in, I beg you, or I'll die.
    Just let me in." And then a peel
Of thunder snuffed it out. The circumstantial

Evidence is plain: I woke with knuckles bleeding,

    My throat dried to a reed, my head concussed.
But just the same, the glowering cloud I'd fought
Was buried deeper in me than all thought:

    My blind and breathless trail an outward husk,
And every fist the self itself exceeding.

IV

Two Verse Letters

Verse Letter to Jason

Take thought:
I have weathered the storm,
I have beaten out my exile.

I am homesick after my own kind.
                    —Ezra Pound

Time was away and somewhere else.
                    —Louis MacNeice

I

It's late in Dublin, Jason. I'm just home
After a few pints at the Bleeding Horse,
Where a century ago, James Clarence Mangan
Drained the last drops of his poetic force.
I couldn't imagine him propped on a stool,
There, enough glasses emptied he could think
His poems taken from O'Hussey or Greek,
Not scribbled forgeries stained dark with drink.
Except for a few charred oak beams, that tavern
Like everything else in this city's altered.

Where Nelson's Pisgah pillar pruned, then plumed,
They've propped a sterile spike up like an altar
To pious E.U. secularity.

    It's getting so Americans can't come
And find their "roots" here anymore than they
Might find them in Seattle or Columbus.
For centuries, unhoused like Hugh Maguire,
"Wandering, without guide or chart," the Irish,
Like you, have learned that filial permanence
Gets inconvenient if you want to die rich.
Not that I care particularly. I would
Prefer to litanies on deracination
A cosmopolitan tract on *Jean Racine:*
His Plays Produced by the Illini Nation.

    Except for the expense, I love it here.
I hate to tour, you know. And though I *should*,
Like every young Midwesterner, believe
Europe's the storehouse of high cultural goods,
I don't. And Dublin is to Europe what Guam
Is to Los Angeles, the moon to Mars,
Their hoof-and-mouth infested cuts of sirloin
To a cold china plate of steak tar-tar.
 Perhaps that's rather much. But this is true:
The salt here has no flavor; pour it on

86

And it just disappears. You know what Our
Lord said of that in Luke . . . Or was it John?

    This, too, is God's own truth, and no one else
But you would understand my simple mind:
I like Dublin simply because I met
A girl. Half Irish, half Maltese, the kind
Of dark hair Mangan must have dreamed of when
He wrote his syrupy verse on Rosaleen.
You wouldn't know that poem from any other—
But if you saw her you'd know what I mean.

    We first spoke passing on the steps of Newman
House; the stone lion watching us from his
Recumbent Georgian pose above the stair like
Desire's image stamped on providence.
She and I passed the next three afternoons
In conversation over carvery
Lunches and pints. I'm not sure what important
Meetings we've missed, but Lady Gregory's
Her favorite writer, and her personal myth
Seems better than those of Kiltartan's Cross.
Nothing I say offends her—but makes her laugh,
And we never speak of leaving or of loss.

    If I said this is *why* I came to Dublin,
Would you believe me? Every general city

Has streets and alleys paved by casual chance,
Yet plotted out in mythic subcommittee.

    But let's leave off with her and maps awhile;
When I had just begun to crawl, you spent
Weeks at a time tucked in a hospital bed,
Bald from the treatments. What was it God meant
In giving you to Mom and Dad, if He
Intended you a short lease and to suffer
Through it? You learned to sob a child's words
As nurses gave you one shot or another.

    My own first memories are of you leaving
Or, smiling, returning from those weeks in Texas.
Because I was so young, I thought your exile
Not one of those dark journeys that affects us
Beyond recovery, but some vacation
From which you always came back. And you came
Bearing beneath the curly wig they fit
You with a galleon full of fictional names.

    If your long hours at Lehman leave you tired,
Too tired to turn the pages of a book
At night, remember that those years ago
Your life seemed saved by tubes and bags on hooks
And occupied by story after story.
Of which I was the beneficiary:

Aside from "God's eyes" made of Popsicle sticks,
You brought the scaled and taloned bestiaries
That made the episodes of heroes' lives
Seem, like Texas, great but unenviable.
Remembering that, would you indulge me now?
I'm far away and have some tales to tell.

II

The best and worst in human nature is
That when we see a man stare down some fate—
A mob of faces fixed, like us, to watch
If his bruised back stiffens or vacillates,
Winning another moment's breath, but losing
His mortal certainty—we wonder why
He's come to this place like a saber's point,
And sit in judgment of his alibi.
So Jason stood on the bare Colchis field;
A wintery stubble and half-unearthed rocks
Cut into his bared foot. The damp dawn air
Blew in from where the pinch-sterned Argos docked.
And every savage servant of Æetes
Shouted advice or jeers from garbled throats
That even the most lonesome Greek would not

Deign to comprehend. He wore his coat
Of leopard skin, scarred leather greaves, and plate
Of tempered bronze mullioned his abdomen.
His hands were empty; he had left his sword
And spear with Peleus and his other men,
And waited for the reins Æetes promised
That yoked two bulls with feet of bronze and breath
That seared the earth with subterranean fires.
With these he'd have to plow the length and breadth
Of the dry field and sow it with dragons' teeth,
Which as the heirs of Cadmus knew, would sprout
Instantly into muted armored soldiers
That he, alone, before the crowd, must rout.
Only then would the king give him what he
Had come for: dead Phrixus' golden fleece.

    Three months before, he'd summoned Castor, Pollux,
The fiercest heroes of the Peloponnese,
And sailed with them. They'd set in at an island
Whose denizens were female parricides.
There, Hylas got sucked under by a dryad;
Hercules vanished in the wood and cried.
Later, they came across Phineus, starved
Down to a whispering shadow of white bone,
Because Zeus sent his harpies to besmirch

His food and leave him, with their stench, alone.
They ended that curse without swords, and rowed
Beneath the rock to which Prometheus
Was bound in chains. They saw the vulture's pass
And heard the god's scream as its talons brushed
His side, anticipating the blood sharp
Beak. Finally, they nearly were immured
By clashing rocks, as they pursued the tail
Of the white pigeon Phineus gave his word
Would guide them through the narrowing passages
Of fate.

       And last night, in his solitude,
Jason had prayed the gods would guard his life.
In darkness, answer came: a girl, half nude,
Offering herself and a clay jar of oil
To make him invulnerable from dawn to dusk.
Here in the burnt and stubbled field he stood,
Impregnable to arrow, sword or tusk.

  Seeing this, do we look back even further
To find Pelius charging him this quest
If Jason would assume his lineal throne
And win the fleece so Phrixus' soul could rest?

  Or should we listen to the murmurs of
Pelius' heart, and think, whatever Jason

Does, this cruel man, when young, usurped the throne
And now he wizens in his paranoid fashion?

    Or do we turn from the smoked glass of time
Expired, to see those doomed kids that Medea
Will bear to Jason, having borne him through
All bloodied obstacles to his gold idea?
Are we required to look upon him now,
Who in his liberty has taken reins
With fearless bravery, and say that his
Will wind up just a cruel, adulterous reign?
Noble dream, old injustice, fated loss
(When, in despair, a mother kills her sons),
These paths of history are presented us
To trace and judge as he turns to meet the sun.

III

    She drew close to the table where we sat
Within the shadow of the clamoring stair.
Her voice, sometimes, was lost within the ring
Of tills and clanking pints. But I could stare
On her, and, should I need to laugh, she'd sign
As much with softening eyes, as if she knew
So long as I could stay this near, no joke

Would fail to please, and all the rendezvous
Of time were just so many shaken hands,
So many names forgot. Dull feet above
Us shook the white rings in our glasses; but,
For all that, all I wanted did not move,
And we rest closer still and still more there,
Beneath the rise and fall of silenced strangers.

IV

You cannot find in that, now—can you?—trace
Of your young brother's typical *sturm und drang*; or
His brief tramontane past that ought to spill
Like poorly packed suitcases down a flight
Of airport stairs, sullied with winter mud.
I hope you *won't,* at least. I'd more recondite
Imaginings intended than to offer
The soft if static sediment of lyric
As yet one more dramatic artifact
Of history's pressure ready for the skeptics'
Unpacking.

            Rather, when the woolen clouds,
Spread sheer against the forenoon sun, grow dark
And soak the stones of Mercer St., tomorrow,

I'll think of that place and pass through the park
At Stephen's Green or down the alley where
The Carmelite Church lets out near Grafton St.
I'll do that for the little while I can:
Both openness and hope make fast retreats
And soon enough are sewn up in the past,
Where indeterminacy grows straight and tight
Like silver thread before the scissors cut.

   That is what made me think of you tonight.
Our memories are moments, by themselves,
But thinking of them, however vague, we feel
That more-than-photographic content pull
The glass and wooden frame away, the sealed
Tableau bleeds backward and bleeds forward—through us.
The image of her lips in disbelief,
I mean, is meaningless unless I've said
Something to set that gesture in relief.

   Think of the time, ten years ago. No. More.
You slouched against the threshold to my bedroom,
Staring at me while I read the pretentious
Novel I'd begged for my birthday. A balloon,
Wilted of helium hung from my bedpost,
And late spring sunlight through the mullioned glass
Patterned mosaic the book, myself, the rug.

You wore, I think, a tee-shirt with your class
Graduation year from Notre Dame
And some small vulgar libel of Dillon Hall;
Your hair was thick still, parted in that wave
Suggesting fastidiousness. My clothes were balled
Up on the bed and off the bed, beneath it.
Save the balloon, when blown up healthily
A decorous blue to show I'd finished high school
And you had got your bachelor's degree,
That moment could've been any moment or
None at all—some scene we weren't meant to know.
But it *was*.

               You leaned there still and bored awhile,
Looked through the linen closet, turned to go,
Before you stood up straight, arms crossed, and said,
With the sincerity of someone who
Has just come from a cousin's funeral—
You said: "Here I am, having finished school;
Having done everything our parents told
Us; having studied what the magazines
Said all the young professionals must know;
Having scored always far above the mean
On every test and tried to look the part
Of some young gentleman whose only itch

Is to beat his great-uncle's handicap,
Be frugal, although infinitely rich."

    And here you stood, survivor of disease
That few survived before you, headed down
To Midland, Texas—place no one had longed
After, place that's no hero's proving ground.

    You had, my brother, done everything right. From
My doorway, every plotted action lay
In place. You checked it over—every turn.
But still you felt condemned in going away
For a few modest promises and coins.
Two moments, both passed, in the night I see,
And wish they could, a moment, just be scenes:
If full of dread, overflowing with possibility.

                        —2003

Verse Letter to My Mother

> But already he's at it
> the form-making proto-maker
> busy at the fecund image of her.
>
> Chthonic? why yes
> but mother of us.
> —David Jones

I

The vines have withered on the garden wall
And snow rests thick enough to weigh the dead
Grass down, leaving the year a pox-marked white.
The stone-eyed angels stare out from seed-beds,
Their pedestals broken, leaned against the shivering
Creepers around which ice has dripped to berries:
Clear skins, white fruit, black pits. When the sun
Has climbed above the branches, it will bury
Such wintery anticipations in
A ground still soft and muddy from a cold
November, till the bracing temperatures
Leave it an easel where the snowy folds
Will stretch like canvas through the darkest months.

My window frames these fallow angels; I
Think how their old conventions have helped me
In writing other verses, as if to ply
An inarticulate thought or two, I need
The sedimentary images of eons,
The interpellations of an enduring past.
To which I add a novel term, like "Freon,"
Or "prestidigitation," or perhaps,
"The internet personal ad filled out by Creon
That sidesteps with a charming, punning joke
His tragic response to what Antigone'd done."
Nothing is made without conventions first
Built in a crumbling wall of mortared stone
To underwrite the sprays of thorn and vine
That could be stripped, but complement its tone.

I think you mentioned years ago that this
Was how all stories worked. I was sixteen (just)
And told you, as you drove me to the dentist,
That I was some imaginative genius
Who needed only time and solitude.
To which you said, "You also need experience."

That was completely wrong, I said, but now
Concede that it has been no small convenience
To live through adolescent hatred, nights

In Boston where my loneliness with books
Seemed like a kind of death, and through the sin
Of mocking what I loved. So, now I look
On all the broken cuckoo clocks, cracked acorns
And springs, the highway billboards that might seem things
Themselves fortuitous and insignificant.
Initiation in their object meanings
Came slow, but certainly began with you.
Not just because you taught me how to read,
But because a boy learns most from watching how
His mother builds the routine world on need;
How winter morning darkness seems an evil
Warded off by the clunk of coffee mugs,
The yawning iron door of the wood stove
As you or Dad replenished it with logs.

   I do not wonder that the story of winter
In the domestic pattern of the seasons,
Tells of a mother gone to save her child
And adds to physical fact symbolic reason.
Nor do I that the winter tale most central
In lives of saints and shoppers—and all others—
Should be an infant's cry in a rank stable,
The means of history born of a mother.

II

What did your mother have to do with Christmas?
The winter you turned ten, she gathered all
Four kids around and said there'd be no gifts,
No tree, or any costly festival.
And so it went. You sat to darn your socks,
Then went to school the next day undistracted
By any usual fantasy of sweets
Or dolls. The time you told me this, you acted
As if it revealed nothing of the care
You took in cutting coupons from the news,
Or loading down our thrifty plastic tree
With ornaments of stars and cockatoos
And filling with odd papered stones the space
Between the floor and wire branches. We
Found Christmas morning all the toys you'd heard
Us adumbrate at length with passing pleas
That otherwise had been forgotten.

       Long

Ago, when Grandma was a little girl,
She and her brothers and her sisters lived
Above their parents' tavern on Blue Isle

In south Chicago. Everyone spoke Polish.
At night, she'd stay up helping grind the beef
And pork for kielbasa. During the day,
The Sisters and the priest without relief
Scolded her use of English. When her mother
Complained, the priest said she was wrong to let
Her daughters lose their holy native tongue.
Polish was all that Grandma would forget.
Her mother told her she must stay in school,
Speak Polish, till her First Communion day.
That was to please her father. After that,
No Mass, no bows to priests; if she would pray,
Her mother said, "you'll do it just as well
At home," where all the family worked and ate
And slept. She never entered church again
Except for on her childrens' wedding dates.

Although her mother saved her then, in a
Few years, my grandma left home, fleeing her
Parents who stole what dollars she had made
At factory work. Her older sisters were
No better; Grandma learned to hoard her cash
In mattresses, in walls, beneath the floor.
The summer after she had died, the workmen
Hired to put her furniture in storeage

Found more than a hundred-thousand dollars packed
Behind the mirror of her vanity.
"She always feared the banks would fail," you said,
But she found more than banks untrustworthy.

   She never stole from you. She would not give,
Of course, clutching tight to her memory;
And everything you asked her, she forbade,
As if the mother so fiercely loyal she
Would take her daughter's side against God lurked
Within the ghost of one quite willing to leave
Her daughter nothing for the pain of work.
Your mother, hers, clenched in their fists their griefs,
And we could hardly say for certain if
They did so to protect the ones they loved
Or if they were on guard against betrayal
From in their home. Or, outside. Or, above.

   Each time I see you, Mother, I think how
Young you look; how, when you left Cicero
To marry, settle near the new-paved streets,
The wide-lawn-punctuating saplings posed
With twine against the summer thunder storms,
Your arms embraced a life both unknown and
Desired. Even now, these forty-one
Years later, you reach out with both your hands

For everything that might have been denied.

   You've told me that a handful of times, on trips
Into the City, Grandpa bought you ice cream
Sandwiched between two waffles. On your lips,
Nothing had tasted richer than the hard
Vanilla melting in the hot sweet squares.
Some weekends, you would bring home chocolate soda
For Jason, John and me, and tell us where
You used to go to buy it after school
With money from your first job: how your eye
Fell on such things, when still a girl, they fall
Still, and within them I can still descry
The greed of a remembered poverty,
Which, to preserve itself, might have harmed us,
Had not delight in things and loyalty
Turned, at last, blessing what had been a curse.

   The day of Grandma's funeral we learned
That in her twenties she'd married and divorced,
And kept the secret more than seventy years.
The husband's name is lost to us, of course,
But this we know: she called the marriage off
Because he didn't want a family, only
Her. Though it was a scandal she would hide,
It retrospectively signs that matrimony

Is more than independent contractors
Who sit at table over *Yung Fu's Wokeries*
And read each other with incredulous smiles
The empty phrases in their fortune cookies
Before retiring to, respectively,
A legal thriller and CNBC.
    Marriage, for her, for all the want of gifts, was
The hope of raising up a family,
The promise that she would not hinder you
Or Connie, John or Jan in happiness
By guarding ceaselessly against excess.
She lived her years in a world she could not bless,
But wanted more than heaven to share it
With the small circle she had formed. If I've
Spent prodigally to resist avarice,
I give now her life not as excuse but tithe.

III

    The frescos in St. Dominic's chapel show
Dimly beneath protective years of dust.
The first is brightly painted, ribboned red
With some young man at court run riotous
And drunk before the woman he would love,

Her face benign or scornfully unaware.
Along the edges, where decay creeps in
Gnawing the grains of paint, there also are,
Watching with dull eyes, four gray devils, who
At first, seem but the accidents of decay.
Each lifts its claw to slash at emblems of the
Virtues the man's forgotten anyway.

    Another shows a studious friar bowed
At prayer, the acrylic of his eyes averted
From the streets of Toulouse, where light and laughter
Rage in the bacchanals of the unconverted.

    A woman gowned in basalt blue and crowned
With the cracked golden nimbus art requires
To interpret in its stillness the extended
Movement toward holiness, extends a briar
Crown dripping five drops of blood to the lady
That drunken lout would love. She takes it close
Against her breast, and in the images
That follow, she is knelt in lachrymose
Meditation on the blood and crown.
We almost certainly are meant to see
Her come to the young man while he's asleep,
Recovering from his decadence, and plead
With his sick soul. Then, in the afternoon,

She explains to him the meaning of the crown
He cannot see, for it is laced about
The wounded pounding of her heart.

                              The sound

Of sexual laughter, silent always here
In the other images, where Dominic
Prays, nonetheless seems loud like horses and trumpets,
While he, in penance beats himself with thick
Cords of rope. In the detail, the saint's blood
Seems separate, super-imposed, as if it were
The real blood of the saint. He's fallen still
Beneath its unrealistic, actual smear.

    The forth detail shows him awake once more.
He has forgot the sacrificial pain
Scored in his back; before him Mary stands.
Her left hand takes his rope, the right contains
The beaded circle of the rosary.

    Visitors to this chapel might find near the door,
If they looked close and it were a real door,
A few lines taken from Louis Montfort:
Mary who came to me, by her faith, come,
Oh Wisdom Heaven-sent that she became.
Come, she who manifests you on the earth,
Yet leaps always upward like a rising flame.

IV

The angels in the yard say nothing till
The mind acts on the secret of their beings,
But we can sense the dormant meanings waiting,
As Dad, when a boy, with his decoder ring
In hand, felt in a fit of nervousness
The long and immanent messages behind
The chain of numbers scratched down on his flip-pad.

These are the images that come to mind,
When I think of you. That I think as well
Not just of you, but mothers generally,
Suggests more than a choice of fierce protector,
Of clannish accidental harm, or the
Transcendent Mediatrix come to guide
Created children through prayer, poetry
And spiritual drama. More than just a choice
Of individual or idolatry.

We sense the singularity of things,
Encounter each as each, but given the time
To know them in their fullness beyond things,
They start to cohere like stanzas out of rhyme:
The world within the made-world comes to being.

And you, my mother, the Rosetta stone,
The messenger, are no iconic paint
Fading upon the wall. You are the one
Who takes the imaginary child inside
The imaginary chapel and shows him
The sequence of small frescos; teaches him
To read the story, make it part of him.

—2005

V

Discipline and Desire

SOLITAIRE

There's cookie dough and chocolate mint stored up
    Next to the untouched vodka in your freezer;
Dead daffodils, whose water grew corrupt
    And brown, have been replaced with new stems tweezered

To last in glass, seem angled but not broken.
    Your neighbors' kids are roaring in the yard,
So I have closed the sliding door. And though, when
    You shut your eyes, I shuffle hush-mouthed cards,

This is no vigil or imprisonment.
    Though you lie weak from all the doctor did
And I play solitaire to pass hours spent
    Watching you wake and sleep and wake in bed,

    Though I had nothing to do with this, I hurt
    You once, and hold you now, to prove I've learned.

SOME PERMANENT THINGS

The retail banker in his cubicle
Will speak of his great-aunt, or cherish clothes
He plucked from her estate sale, with some dull
Soporifics so quaint they can't be posed.
But jealous of the little powers his branch
Manager gives like souvenir coffee cups,
He drops the sweet talk—as Acton says, corrupt—
To charge this late fee or repossess that ranch.

Inclined to think the salesman's smile cheap paint,
The earnest confidence less pearl than swine,
And every pinned lapel a scoundrel's feint,
We bathe our sentiments in turpentine;
Suspect adultery in our neighbor's nest;
Leave love and faith in nursing homes to rot
Where they feed on those innards we forgot;
And mock our innocence for its hollow chest.

But discontented sipping irony,
The occasional citizen will hear a drum
Sounding with more than antique vibrancy.

He wanders through the alleys till he comes
Upon an old flag in the collective attic:
Too plain for casual appreciation,
Enduring every age's violation,
Its crest grown true, more bloody, and more vatic.

THE NEW LIFE

For Hilary

Though neither young nor old, nor full of wine,
  Not blind, exactly, though my sight was poor,
I crouched, a beggar waiting for a sign
  So obvious the dead could not ignore.

A *flâneur* so much as is possible
  In a despoiled city such as this,
Amid the listless crowd, I casually strolled,
  Searching for a stare not quite purposeless.

A bibliographic recluse in his room,
  I "mused," what word could make me close my book.
Some Old West drunk passed out by the spittoon,
  What patient face could cure me with a look?

  Then you came—sign, stare, cure, and word—and brought
  A new life where none was but one was sought.

A PRAYER FOR LIVIA GRACE

There's little room left in this house for poetry,
Or in this world for any lasting language.
The managers and sales reps in the office
Who've ticketed their holidays are childless,
And looking toward five days of sun and liquor.
They care for neither old books nor a young daughter.

But somehow near me sleeps an infant daughter
Who grows still to the cradle sounds of poetry,
Eyelids dropped in the promise of sleep's liquor.
It charms her, yet she knows nothing of language;
Nor did I, in a way, when I was childless,
Preoccupied with filling another office

Than fatherhood. Now crowded in my office,
A crib and chest of pink drawers for my daughter
Remind me that this empty room sat childless
Except for those ink-littered sheets of poetry,
When "child" was just a word and my child language,
Which I would write and read at night with liquor.

Now she's born, we have little time for liquor
And my desk's crammed in a corner of the office,
My papers lost beneath the brighter language
Of cardboard colored alphabets for my daughter.
I'm sure I wrote a different kind of poetry
When all my hours were filled though I was childless.

The TV news shows that, because they're childless,
Exercise, and shun cigarettes and liquor,
Modern consumers live a life of poetry:
Controlled and self-absorbed as fits the office
Of sonnets or sestinas; their only daughter
An *iPod* or such ephemeral techno-language.

I pray, my daughter, speak another language,
That in the richest sense you not be childless,
Your every act a kind of lasting daughter
More beautiful than bored clerks at their liquor.
Though they find no room for it at the office,
May you crowd your small corridors with poetry.

My daughter's teething, needs her gums rubbed with liquor,
Which stops my language, calls me from my office.
I go. May I have more of this child, less poetry.

At the Public Pool

The lifeguard stretches to pull off her tee-shirt,
  Unveiling the white cross taut on her breasts,
  The sunlight oiled in her shoulders, smothered
In her hair. Two retirees take a rest
  Beneath the picnic parasols, unbothered
  By supine teens on cell phones jawing at leisure.

But far from all the squeals and bone-white splashes,
  The pastel-flowered inner-tubes and swimsuits
  Bobbing the blue glass of the public pool,
My daughter watches, wades waist deep on thin shoots
  Of legs that wobble in the kiddy pool's
  Bright circle. A group of older children passes,

Skirting the lounge chairs en route to the deep
  Beyond. But she clings tenuous to this shallow,
  Ventures a patting palm against its surface,
A reach back to the concrete edge, so she'll know
  Where I and safety sit. I look on her face
  And guess that only the soft blank of sleep

Will bring her back the laughing recklessness
    Lost when, a quarter hour ago, she slipped
    And dropped face-forward through the water's plain
Into a silent world of light, whose grip
    Held her in thrall until undone by mine.
    Did she, a moment, feel that long caress

Toward which we're pulled and which we can resist?
    The tanned, bikinied lifeguard stared at me,
     The soft dark of her thigh another lure
Into another kind of fatality.
    I clutched my daughter, but my eyes searched *her*,
    And dreaded what, a moment, I could wish.

A Note for Ecclesiastes

In Memoriam Rae Lee Lester

I

The parson, lonely in his vicarage
At Bemerton, sits over his book of proverbs.
He wonders what outlandish phrase might shake
The wind-burned, inarticulate assurance
Of farmers gathered in the pews: to teach them
That summer need not follow winter, wealth
Might never sooth their labors, that the seeds
They scattered with their children, when the earth
Grew soft and damp in memories of ice,
Need not sprout into corn. How does one stir
A dull eye to the poignancy and gift
Of all the things that are but need not be?

He'll get no help from ancient meditations,
The maxims of a general in Gaul.
The snow upon the woods, the ice upon
The Danube, all the broken swords and bodies
Unburied in the quiet, conquering dusk:
"These things have always been, and will again,

In boundless space and endless generations,"
He wrote, and turned his horse's steaming snout
Back toward the marble monuments of Rome.

II

There are too many of them, all the wise:
The weak sententious men grown drunk on scotch,
The flint-lipped quietists, the smug advisor
Certain no treasonous plot, utopian scheme,
Or menu in an obscure restaurant
Contains a newborn thought, a hope that hasn't
Been crushed before—in more auspicious times;
No kiss bestowed with awkward tenderness is
A new page in the history of love.

And you, Ecclesiastes, you, the first
To wipe the settled dust from off his hands
And cry between the river and the sea
That all is ancient, all is vanity,
That nothing under the dry sun is new:
No agony of joy; nothing, nothing,
Not even the light of falling stars is new.

III

But we are here not to consent, abashed,
To those who found a city in the sand—
And called it dull. We come not to admire
Those singular wits who see in naive lovers
The venomous shades of old, unhappy marriages.
We're not here to attest that we have seen
The troubled, fertile constancy of seasons,
Or slothful regularity of stars.
We come to mourn that in some old crone's stitch work,
Or in the curtains of our living room,
There's been a tear. Right here. A hole has formed
And it will not be mended. I say again,
There's been a tear; and no needle's wisdom we
Can thread, no sonorous lessons in disinterest,
Can tell us that the woman we have lost
Has been before, or that another like her—
With a like voice, perhaps, or the same hair—
Will fill this emptiness she occupied.

We do not need a shaking from our comfort
In how the seasons feed us, how the new
Wars are just like the old ones. What we ask

121

Is wisdom wise enough never to dare
To try to take the measure of our loss.
We do not need to know all things have been,
But only to say, once more and in fitting
Voice, that she was.

THE FIRST SUNDAY OF ADVENT

The weight of steel against the heaving rails,
Those strict rust parallels
Between the platforms, where commuters stand
In topcoats, mufflers, or in woolen hats:
Numb fingers thumbing the loose ends
      Of gloves, expectant of the call
To draw them from their winter suburbs off
To the iced towers of the working daylight.

We have some hope once other hopes have failed:
Raise trees that have been felled;
The blank cashier who answers our command
For coffee and a scone. We feel the fat
Of idle hours, the long feline
      Stretch of life's sabbatical.
Our eyes are set toward Center City; aloft,
The southerly birds head toward an age of daylight.

But when? the glorious letter in the mail
With words of rustling bells?
When? the permanent heat in the cold land?

Our limbs are aching and our feet are flat,
Our thoughts encumbered by the gravitas
        Of each body's weight. Our fall
Was hard and like no other. Will the soft
Wing of some other life lift us toward daylight?

The Second Sunday of Advent

In the warm circle of lamplight, my daughter
Reaches up toward the pocket stitched with "8"
For silver wrapped chocolate stowed there. As I've taught her,
She may eat one each night, and each night waits

For my return from work with hungry eyes.
Her joy is regulated thus: a prayer,
A story, and a candy. Then, she cries
To get but one when there are others there.

St. Augustine, knowing the greed of babes for
Their mothers' breasts was violent and abyssal,
Confessed that infant innocence was made more
Of helpless limbs than grace, less rose than thistle.

My daughter takes the unwrapped sweet and chews
With a slow-smackeral ritual I admire.
The past had little purity to lose;
And we have only discipline and desire.

FROM THE TRINITY CAPITAL

For Hilary

Beyond the purple velvet drapes, the skeins
Of billowed gossamer, my hotel window
Looks down on the back gates of Trinity
College. Up three floors and pierced by a late
October sun, the room has been done up like
A swinger's pad, with leopard print and leather,
With mirrors and conic shaded lights in orbit
About the dark mass of the pillowed bed.
This style was once regrettable. And now:
Now, all regrets are off. Tour buses crowd
Streets pounded, once, with fire from a British
Gun ship; wide streets once packed with bowlered clerks
Hastening to catch the train back to Roscommon
For Easter.
              Two women, with whom I shared a cab
In from the airport, stared out at the palms
Grown in front gardens, shading Georgian doors,
And waited for some ginger-headed priest
Or pink-nosed drunk to trundle down the road.
My room's a tiger of prosperity,
Designed by someone so assured that now

The exile ship and Eucharistic Congress
Are past, a buried fashion can be flirted
With; someone who would never understand
Why the tourist from Schaumburg or Roxbury
Would hustle past the brushed steel of the hotel
Bar, off to have a pint in Wicklow or
Sit down for tea and fry while sight-seeing Tara.
Why should the Polish maid in the corridor
Regret that things turned out this way? Here where
The sorrowed past was only lately lost?

    It's four years now since I last saw these streets,
Since I decided to move home, and since
I gave up on some other love, some other
Life, winding up in South Bend—and met you.
This city's swelled with luck, and I could wish
It otherwise: the vomit in the late bars,
And ads for XXX on pay TV
That vend to hotel guests their "burning passions."
The fields of Ireland have always wished
Things had been different—or that they were now.

    Hilary, the mind obsessed with its own powers
Pretends that this or that decision, words
Called out to a shy woman in the dark
Of summer, with the river sounds, the sounds

Of drunken chatter and the swinging gate,
Might be unsaid, the rusting hinges shut,
Unknown. There may be many things undone,
About which I may think though they'll not be,
As if they were lead figures on a board,
Subject in their position to my scrutiny.
But some thoughts said—once said—are sacraments;
They can't be unconceived or lived without.
The great impossible is to unthink the path
And fortune's fleet missteps that carried me on it,
That brought me to you, and you within my mind
To dwell as the immobile real called love.

    Because of the odd shock, I've sometimes said,
"Had I stayed here, I'd not have met you"; but
No counter-factual alternate course in time
Seems less real. For, your actual love and being
Have made their print so firmly that I can
Neither think of a life without you nor
Quite think without your presence looming up:
Always, your eyes beneath dark hair, your voice
Rising with singular certainty to greet
Me in the silent rooms of every city.

VI

VERSE LETTER TO JOHN

Some artists, and I am one of them, wish to live and work within a community, or within the hope of community, in a given place. Others wish to live and work outside the claims of community, and these now appear to be an overwhelming majority.

   —Wendell Berry

One of the first symptoms they discover of a selfish and mischievous ambition, is a profligate disregard of a dignity which they partake with others. To be attached to the subdivision, to love the little platoon we belong to in society, is the first principle (the germ as it were) of public affections. It is the first link in the series by which we proceed towards a love to our country and to mankind.

   —Edmund Burke

I

It's August 1ˢᵗ in Greenville, nearly Midnight,
And we have sacrificed to the hearth gods—
Of whom we took possession earlier
Today, with the uneasy smile and nod
Young couples signing mortgages display
To accept without quite grasping the strict words
Of lawyers, and to endure our being bound
To banks that will outlive us. We have poured
A bottle of our Michigan Riesling, drunk
It quickly to bear up amid the sense
That ownership of house, a plot of land,
The mice and leaking faucet, broken vents,
All walls in need of spackle and fresh paint,
May turn out to own us instead. We thought
To celebrate, propitiate, but now
Half beg forgetfulness of what we've wrought.
    What's more, the tastes of mineral in the wine
Conjured for Hilary the land and loves
That we have left behind for this burnt South.
We've traded them for fire ants, work gloves
To clean dead roaches and mouse droppings, and

Stacked photos of the old owners—all their junk
Left moldering in an humid attic crawl space
Ours by signed deed alone. I hauled a trunk
Out to the curb this afternoon, packed dense
With Christmas baubles, school work, a salt map
Textured to show the Carolina terrain.
To someone this was home; to us it's crap,
Or perhaps worse: crude omens it takes years
To fit a place for lasting happiness,
But even given proper time the task miscarries
Often enough and leaves a hoarded mess
Littered or pawned-off rather than forgotten.

 But drink we did, and watched *The Quiet Man*:
The TV on the hearthstone; us reclined
On an inflated mattress. The show began,
Kindling in blue our hollowed living room
With neither couch nor lamp, nor pictures hung,
And it beat back a bit the alien dark,
Rooting us where we felt we had been flung.

 Soon Hilary and Livia were asleep,
The latter pressed into her mother's side,
And I am left to think, within this place
John Wayne and another steady pour provide,
Of outlets, stairs, and days of child-proofing;

Of fire ant hills that have us under siege;
Of hunger for the places we called home;
To wish the walls were painted white or beige;
To wonder if this house to which we're tied
Will prove a hearth- or millstone; and to write
You, John, the oldest, first of all to marry,
The one most given to think and do what's right
In the eyes of parents, customers, and State.
It's you I think of now, I want to know
Not merely how to jimmy painted windows
But what goes in the making of a home.

II

These mornings in September start out cool,
As I take my leave from the slumbering house
And head to campus. On the road, I'm joined
By rural women in their name-tagged blouses,
By dark-skinned migrants without names, who flood
In from the trailer parks and distant villages
Circling town. They come to work the counters
And building sites for low, illegal wages,
As lot by lot old farmers sell their fields
To found new suburbs in the sand expanses

Punctuated by strip-malls and "drive-thrus"
Developers throw up with reckless glances.
  I come to the bright center, ringed in neon
Signs, old farm houses and the marginal shacks,
To where the busses drop off students: dull,
Confused, maybe, unsure how they were tracked
For college, knowing only that they've come
And found the lite beer flowing, courses hard,
And the whole landscape scrawled with purple slogans
About the future's prospects. The past is barred
To them, or rather buried underneath
The asphalt of the Food Lion parking lot,
Their guidance counselors' tripe of laboring freedom,
And sneers at rural idiocy. No plot
Of ploughed earth for these students, only tales
Of air-conditioned clinics, steady checks,
Of keyboard clicks, and nursing scrubs succeeding
The bent-backed grandparents whose beams were wrecked
Last summer to make room for a new PricePharm.
  It is at this space I arrive each day,
Skirting the fire ant mounds to hurry through
A glassy education factory,
Remembering that final sort of sneer
Kirk made, when he resigned a post like mine,

Against the rationalizing circus tamers
Whose trained behemoth, open-jawed and blind,
Promised to carry to prosperity
The young of generations in her stomach.
    From deep inside, I greet my students' blank
Faces, intone with gravid voice this *one* ache
For the inherited order our age sold:
"And surely never lighted on this orb
A more delightful vision, a morning star
That this dark revolution would absorb.
The age of chivalry is gone; and that
Of sophisters, œconomists, and bond-hacks
Succeeds to overturn our proud illusions
With superstitions of the social contract."
The rustle of bored bodies—silenced by
This cry ventriloquized—makes slow return,
As the hour ends and they herd off to Business
Aps. I'm left with my textbooks, to discern
If shoring rhetoric against these ruins
Amounts to just a little phlegm or bile
Unsettled in the beast that welcomes it,
My bit of chalk a dusty sword, even while
Progress through easy credit lets its stream
Flow placid, dark, and ever deeper. Did Burke

Sate necessary loss with scribal flourishes,
Masking in righteousness mere party work?
    Would he have strolled out from the lectured dark
To greet the baked air of the afternoon
With snarls for both the sprawled efficiency
And the remunerative dreaming of those soon-
To-be-employed and landless former sons?
They swell in from that country which their fathers
Fought to wall off from any wind of doctrine
Or foreign army. These students swear another
Vow no less resolute: to mold themselves
Into the faithful representatives
Of the new market as it melts to air.
Among them, I *de facto* come to live,
And like them fit my doctrines and desires
To those most practical of ends: to pay
The mortgage, keep the table spread, forestall
The moral reckoning another day.

III

The All Saints Vigil Mass, here at Saint Peter's,
Has ringed its belled way to the consecration,
The pews swelled with the zealous newly baptized
Who kneel and pray. Much to my consternation,
I sit with Livia in the muted closet
That serves as parish cry-room till the funds
Come through for needed renovations. Livia
Practices walking, teetering among
The clutch of empty chairs, her teary fit
Just dried. Upon the wall, a cross and icon
Of the Theotokos and a television
Whose grainy screen reveals the priest—his mic. on
To static forth like shook tin through blown speakers,
"Supper ended, he took the cup. Again
He gave you thanks and praise . . ." I see the chalice
Raised up, and through the wall the Great Amen
I hear: the hymning of the faithful stirring
The modern stone foundations.
                                        Like a frame
About the screen, rise crooked shelves, some bowed
Beneath their weight of myriad books with flames,

Cross-sceptered orbs, and fleur-de-lis imprinted
Upon the spines, along with names like Knox
And Sheen, Gheon and Maritain, de Sale,
Chautard, and others—familiar yet locked
Away, the property of another age.
Cracked but long unopened, their plain designs
Are like the dim unpeopled shrines of Amherst,
South Bend, or Somerville, where I would find
Myself the solitary youth knelt by
The hunched and hushed retirees at prayer:
Those who remembered trains of priests behind
The monstranced Host as incense smoked the air.
They'd tasted of that rational confidence,
Devotion scripted to precision, walls
Of flame-lit marble worthy to receive
The flesh of Christ called down, to withstand the calls
Of the crass, mercantile restlessness
Waiting out in the streets. Who could have seen
That order would be hollowed out? That all
This well-turned apologia would cease to mean,
Its popular scholasticism silenced—
Left foxed, forgotten on a cry-room shelf?

    Our family heard both voices, I now think:
Our grandpas who, in their way, died to self,

The one through draining charity, the other,
Who planned to join the priesthood till he met
That star of joy and bitterness upon
A ballroom floor and married her. Don't forget
The seminarian who came to dinner
To help you to discern; you turned apostle
Soon after and with fervor more enduring
To the shrewd props of Ronald Reagan's gospel.

How long, how very much longer, I was haunted
By that vocation to sublimity
And self-forgetting, that ascent of mind,
Is hard to say. In retrospect, I see
Me driven from decision to decision,
Each one worse than the last, as I fled from
The one delight I did not dare, and found
Myself with wife and child—my calling come
In spite of me. We mark, like trailed-off noises
Of drum and trumpet from a Feast parade,
Those generations who saw in the Church the
Perfect Society, that union made
By revelation of the intellect
And painted piety, so that the world
Found its apt symbol in a Virgin's heart.
Now, all those marching banners have been furled.

Now, I see all the enigmatic faces
Turned to our priest, upon the cry-room screen.
Some have come, hoping to recover what's
Not lost but shelved, while others may not mean
To, but, with their *soupçons* of jazz and rock,
Their salesman's smiles and hugs at the kiss of peace,
Sow not old seeds anew but graft strange roots
Less sacred if no less sincere.
                                        I cease
This wandering, snatch up Livia, and head out
To join the overflowing communion line
Uncertain what these groans of birth and death
Import, but pleading they not make her blind,
When she has eyes matured to see, that here
Alone, despite the kitsch and clutter, here
Alone do body, home, and city last,
As the Incarnate Word redeems our fears.

IV

I hear from Mom it's snowing in Michigan
And that you two are coming with the boys
Thanksgiving Day. We're all glad for such times:
To set aside the calculus of joys

And wants, of life as a rights-tattooed body
In search of profits, pleasures, and protection.
We rest on rock, and think, just then, that sea
Of nameless faces are our neighbors. Reflection
On gifts and thankfulness reveals another
Self to us, not the one we choose, create,
Or crown as our one certitude; but one
That lives only because he's loved, whose state
Is given not by contract but as are
The Auroras up North to accepting eyes.
We drink the light by nature not demand.

    Was it to such creaturely verities
That Reagan called us, now three decades back?
He spoke of restoration and of duty,
Not the sort that sugars and cans Fall fruit,
But sails at morning out in search of booty.
Whatever the intent, you found a discipline
And honor in his words that's served you well
And brought you home and wife and family—more
Than anyone deserves or I could tell.

    Our history's overcrowded with the rhetoric
Of national splendor, missions to the moon
Or Middle East, as if we only care
For what is ours when challenged at high noon.

But we are subjects of a Kingdom greater
Than any rocket could cross or control
And in whose glory we receive what's given.

    What's given is a more fragile, humble role
Than technocrats with social plans might like.
The Lord of History gives his subjects homes
In a particular country: where we live
Best when we cultivate and refuse to roam.
We give thanks in stewardship for what's not ours,
To curb the fire ants and plant the soil,
To help our neighbor mend his backyard fence:
Like Benedict, we live by prayer and toil.
By prayer and toil, John, we try to found
In unfamiliar land grounds to rejoice:
A doubtful task, but one we have received,
A certain blessing, to which this note gives voice.

—2007

James Matthew Wilson is the author of two chapbooks of poems, *Four Verse Letters* (Steubenville, 2010) and *The Violent and the Fallen* (Finishing Line, 2013), of *Timothy Steele: A Critical Introduction* (Story Line Press, 2012), and of many poems, essays, articles, and reviews. An award-winning scholar of philosophical-theology and literature, he is Associate Professor of Humanities and Augustinian Traditions at Villanova University and lives in the village of Berwyn, Pennsylvania, with his wife and children.

Acknowledgments

Versions of most of these poems first appeared in various journals and magazines: "Some Permanent Things" and "Beyond Gibraltar" in *The Dark Horse*; "The Mishawaka Cruisers" and "From the Trinity Capital" in *The Raintown Review*; "Alone, Far from the *New Yorker*," "The Vineyard Dinner: A Retrospect," "Not Yet, Not Yet," and "To N.H." in *Lucid Rhythms*; "Balloon Man," "Their Time up at State College," "Acedia" and "Verse Letter to My Father" in *The Bend*; "A View from the Studebaker's Servants' Quarters" and "The Gypsies" in *Chronicles*; "Living Together" in *Per Contra*; "*Et in Arcadia Ego*" in *First Things*; "Immigrant Serving Maid in Dublin," "From a Bench in St. Stephen's Green," "Drink, Drink," and "Bunches of Blackberries" in *Measure*; "At Father Mac's Wake," "The New Life," "A Note for Ecclesiastes," and "The Second Sunday of Advent" in *The Publican of Philadelphia*; "A Prayer for Livia Grace" in *Modern Age*; "At the Public Pool," "Nevermore," "Lyric," and "Essay on Education" in *Think*; "The First Sunday of Advent" in *Vineyards*; "Barnum," "Dark Places," "To the Reader," and "*Physique de la mort*" in *Dappled Things*; "The Book of Nature I" in *Front Porch Monthly*; "Yeats in London" and "Of Correspondences" in *Notre Dame Review*; "The Book of Nature II" in *Able Muse*; "Old Man in a Café" in *Connotations*; "Solitaire" in *Roman Catholic Arts Review*; and "*De Profundis*" in *The St. Austin Review*.

The Verse letters "To My Father," "To Jason," "To My Mother," and "To John" were first published together in the chapbook *Four Verse Letters* (Franciscan University at Steubenville Press, 2010), and most of the poems appearing in sections I and V first appeared in the chapbook *The Violent and the Fallen* (Finishing Line Press, 2013).

143

37573819R00089

Made in the USA
Lexington, KY
07 December 2014